The Magic Gourd

RETOLD AND ILLUSTRATED BY • Baba Wagué Diakité • A WEST AFRICAN FOLKTALE

SCHOLASTIC INC.
New York Toronto London Auckland Sydney
Mexico City New Delhi Hong Kong Buenos Aires

ISBN 0-439-74696-5

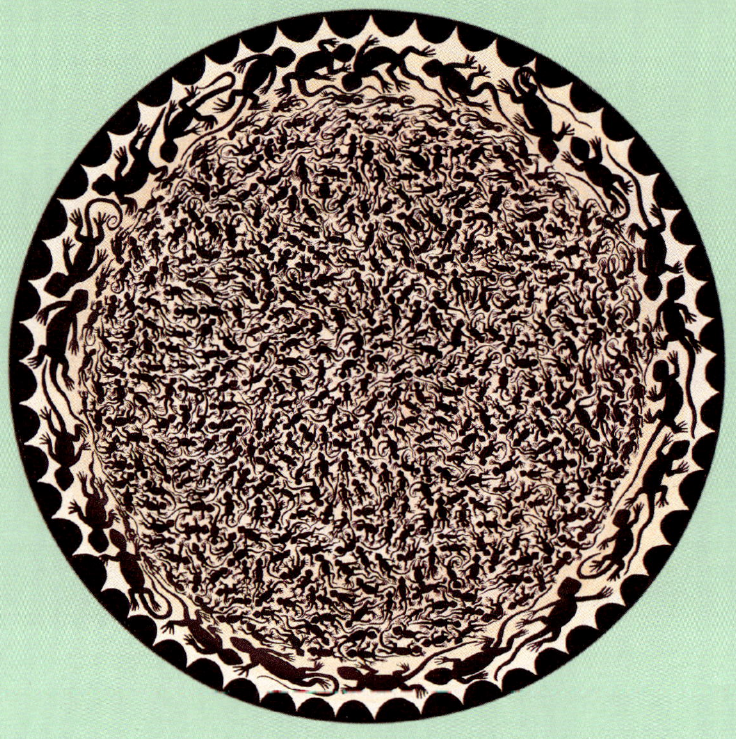

12 11 10 9 8 7 6 5 4 3 2 1　　　5 6 7 8 9 10/0

Printed in the U.S.A.　　　08

First Scholastic paperback printing, January 2005

The text was set in CG Colage. The display was set in Angryhog ITC. Wagué's art was created from ceramic plates, bowls, and tiles. The chameleon is a hand-built clay sculpture. The mud cloth on the dedication page was designed by Baba Wagué Diakité and executed by Seydou Coulibaly. The mud cloth on the endpapers was designed and executed by Seydou Coulibaly. Wagué's art was photographed by Aaron Johanson and Leo Arfer. The back cover photo is by Leo Arfer. Book design by Kristina Albertson and Marijka Kostiw

Special thanks to Karen Van Rossem and Libby Tucker for their help in leading us to early versions of this tale.

For those who have little,
Yet live a life of utmost grace—
This book is dedicated to the people of Mali.

IT ALL BEGAN

when the sun refused to allow the clouds to gather, and there was no rain. First came drought. Then came famine. Everyone was hungry. And it was then that Brother Rabbit wandered around the parched countryside searching for wild roots to feed his starving family. As he walked, he sang . . .

Feeyeh ku, feeyeh ku. Waara sa kun tay.

Luck will come. Life will be good.

Suddenly, Rabbit was interrupted by a sweet little voice that called out, "Dogo Zan! Dogo Zan! Rescue me from this thorny bush! My arms are being poked and scratched! Help me, and I will pay you well."

Rabbit was busy, but still he stopped. "I will help simply to avoid seeing my brother suffer," said Rabbit. Gently he lowered his hand between the thorny branches and saved the green chameleon. As Rabbit turned to leave, Chameleon called out to him once again.

“Dogo Zan! Don’t go yet! Would you mind getting my gourd from the bush, too?”

“A gourd?” cried Brother Rabbit. “You want me to scratch myself again for a little gourd?”

“Please, Dogo Zan,” begged Chameleon. “I will reward you well.”

Again, Rabbit’s kind nature got the best of him, and he bent into the thorny bush and rummaged around.

Rabbit brought out a beautifully decorated gourd and handed it to Chameleon. But Chameleon just said, “Keep it. It’s your reward.”

“It’s just an empty gourd,” Rabbit cried.

“It’s not *just* an empty gourd,” Chameleon replied. “It’s MAGIC!”

“Ee ko dee!” cried Rabbit. “A magic gourd?”

“Oh, yes!” said Chameleon. “Watch this: Magic Gourd, fill yourself up with insects!”

Brother Rabbit watched in amazement as Chameleon licked up a bowl full of insects.

“Why are you giving me such a valuable gift?” Rabbit asked.

"You were kind to me, Brother Rabbit," Chameleon said. "Besides, I have my own secret for catching insects," and he quickly unrolled his lo-o-o-o-o-ong tongue for Rabbit to admire.

Rabbit thanked Brother Chameleon and rushed home with his gourd.

As soon as he arrived home, his entire family eagerly gathered around.

"An empty gourd?" they all gasped in disbelief.

"It's not *just* an empty gourd," said Brother Rabbit. "It's a magic gourd! Watch this: Magic Gourd!" he said. "Fill yourself up with carrots!"

To their astonishment, the gourd magically filled with carrots. Happily, they ate them all.

"Magic Gourd! Fill yourself up with couscous!" he said.

Again they ate until they were satisfied.

"Magic Gourd! Fill yourself up with water!" he said, and they drank deeply.

From that day on, Brother Rabbit's family drank and ate well.

But as much as they wanted to keep the magic gourd a family secret, they also could not sit and watch friends and neighbors suffer. So they invited them to share their meals every day.

And this is how word floated around from one to the other until it came to the house of Mansa Jugu, the greedy king.

One day, the greedy king and his soldiers broke into Rabbit's compound and forced the little gourd away from him. Now, with the magic gourd in his possession, Mansa Jugu sat day and night commanding the little gourd to fill and refill with more and more gold.

Meanwhile, unable to get the magic gourd back, Rabbit returned once again to his poor life, scrounging for wild roots to feed his hungry family. Despite the hardships of the moment, he still had courage to sing . . .

Feeyeh ku, feeyeh ku. Waara sa kun tay.

Luck will come. Life will be good.

One day, while hunting for roots, Rabbit heard his name being called again.

"Dogo Zan, Dogo Zan!"

Recognizing the sweet little voice, he turned and looked in all directions. Slowly the chameleon came into view right next to him on a sparkling green rock.

"Dogo Zan! What has happened to you?" cried Chameleon. "You look skinny and pathetic!"

Rabbit told him all about the greedy king who stole the gourd. Again, Brother Chameleon offered a gift to Brother Rabbit. This time, it was the beautiful crystal rock he had been standing on.

"What is this, Brother Chameleon?" asked Rabbit.

"This is just a *fara*, a little rock!" As soon as the words came out of his mouth, the rock leaped into the air and bounced off his head.

"*Eee-heeeee! Fara!*" cried Rabbit. "Stop! Stop!"

Again, the rock knocked his head.

"Excuse me, Dogo Zan," said the chameleon. "You must call him by his name, *Fara-Ba!*" With that, the rock dropped silently to the ground. Rabbit thanked Chameleon for this unusual gift and returned home.

The next day, Brother Rabbit rolled the rock in a fresh *sheeyo* leaf and walked to the king's palace. "I have brought you a mysterious gift, your Majesty," said Brother Rabbit.

"Aaa ha! Moondon! What is it?" asked the king anxiously. Rabbit slowly unrolled the rock from the *sheeyo* leaf and showed it to Mansa Jugu.

"Eeeeeeh! Fara doron?" exclaimed the king. "A simple rock?"

And with that, the little rock began ricocheting off the head of the king. "*A toh! A toh!* Stop this rock!" cried the king, but no one could capture it. All day and all night the little rock played music on the heads of the king and his soldiers. The annoyance continued and the king became troubled. Mansa Jugu was finally forced to call on Rabbit for help.

Cleverly, Brother Rabbit demanded his little gourd back first.

"You may take all the gold, but leave me the gourd," said the greedy king.

"But the gourd was a gift to me," replied Rabbit.

"Then take all my food from my royal storage bins, but leave me the gourd," cried the annoyed king.

"*Ee dusu dah*. Let us bargain," countered Rabbit. "My little gourd is my prize."

The king angrily shouted, "*U-TAH, U-TAH*—TAKE IT ALL! Take the gold, the food, and the little gourd!"

Rabbit took the gourd, but left the gold and the food behind. And before he turned to flee, he shouted, "*Fara-Ba!*"

Calmly, the little rock dropped into Rabbit's hand.

Fearing revenge from the king, Rabbit's family escaped to the country to join their faithful friend Chameleon. From Chameleon's great lessons in disguises, Brother Rabbit learned the skill of hiding in the bush. Today Dogo Zan and his family are masters at going undetected. One could be hiding

in your backyard

right now.

Mansa Jugu, the greedy king, and his soldiers felt embarrassed by their defeat at the hand of a rabbit and a small rock. The king could not believe that in his moment of weakness, he had given away the wealth of his kingdom. Exhausted and hungry, the king sat down to eat before pursuing Brother Rabbit for revenge. Upon opening his storage bins, he was surprised to discover that all of his wealth and food remained.

"Come eat!" he called to his soldiers and servants. "Let us appreciate what we have been given."

From this final kind act of Rabbit, the greedy king, Mansa Jugu, began to learn the importance of generosity and friendship.

As for Rabbit and Chameleon, they have always understood that loyal friendships are the true treasures that make one rich.

And for their many good deeds, all sang a

song of praise to Rabbit and Chameleon.

A Song of Praise

Bamfula be cheba do fay,	A person may have a beautiful hat,
O tay dana maa yay.	But still, he may be unworthy.
Dulokiw be cheba do fay,	A person may wear beautiful clothes,
O tay dana maa yay.	Yet still, he may be unworthy.
Samaraw be cheba do fay,	A person may wear beautiful shoes,
O tay dana maa yay.	Yet he may still be unworthy.
Nafolo bau be cheba do fay,	A person may have a pocket full of money,
Dambay ti la.	Yet if he is unworthy, he has no wealth.

This praise song may have been the one that was sung to Rabbit and Chameleon at the end of the story. It explains that material wealth is not important, but spiritual wealth is a person's most valuable possession.

Songs of praise are important in Mali. When a gift is received, the recipient will announce it, going from person to person, then door to door in the compound to draw others into acknowledging a kindness that was done. The giver receives thanks from everyone. So the act of sharing and giving gifts makes the giver the wealthiest of all, as the thanks, praise, and acknowledgment they receive from others become gifts as well.

For generations, the *djeliw* (jell-LEEU), or oral historians in Mali and throughout West Africa, have kept and broadcast the good acts of kings and heroes through praise songs that keep the memory of these actions alive today. When we compliment, appreciate, and respect one another, we create a better community.

A person will die, but the spirit of his or her good deeds will live forever.

Author's Note

As a child growing up in the country of Mali, West Africa, I was sent to my grandparents in the village of Kassaro to join my brothers, sisters, and cousins for our traditional education. At first it was hard. I knew I would miss my parents. But soon I felt like an important part of this bigger family, and I enjoyed sharing the responsibilities of everyday life with my siblings and cousins. We helped our grandmother in her garden and our aunts and uncles in their fields, and we tended to the sheep and goats. We had a lot of fun, also, discovering how to make our own toys with millet stalks, sticks, and wire we would scavenge.

At the evening meal, everyone was present in the compound—grandparents, aunts, uncles, and all the children. We shared our food as we gathered around the community bowls. Afterward, in the darkening hours, stories would be told around the fire. Sometimes these would be folktales reflecting situations in our daily lives, teaching us the right path to take. My favorites were always the stories about *Zozani* (zoh-zah-NEE) the rabbit. Rabbit stories are very popular among children in Mali. Because Rabbit always plays a clever role in stories, every child would like to identify himself as Rabbit. I still like Rabbit stories, even as an adult. I love sharing them with others, too!

As a shepherd boy, spending solitary days in the bush gave me time to reflect upon the messages transmitted in the stories of the previous night. I shared my meals of wild fruits and roots with the animals around me. The presence or absence of certain animals forecast the seasons' changes to me. This told me when and where to move my herds. The rocks and termite mounds became my guides to different areas. When I recognized my landmark "friends," I would feel at home once more. This was how I began to understand the importance of nature and of sharing our world with the other animals who live with us.

On moonlit nights, other forms of stories took place through dances and songs. Many songs were songs of praise.

Mud Cloth Patterns

The borders on the tiles and platters in this book are designs taken from traditional *bogolanfiniw* (bo-go-lahn-FEE-neew), or mud cloth. Mud cloth is a unique textile technique of the Bamana people of Mali. The designs, which are painted with dark mud on treated woven cotton cloth, have meanings associated with them. Some depict historic events or well-known people. I have used traditional mud cloth patterns as border designs throughout this book. Some were taught to me by my mother. They are used in places that are meaningful to the story. Their meanings are as follows:

PAGE 6 – These patterns, "The Iguana's Elbow" and "The Square," signify initiative and integrity.
PAGE 7 – "The Chameleon's Tail" signifies adaptability.
PAGE 8 – The pattern on the gourd exterior, "The Battle Between Samory and Tieba," recalls a historic battle between two kings in southern Mali. The main pattern depicts the fortress wall of Tieba's town of Sikasso.
PAGE 10 – "House of Children" signifies a happy family.
PAGE 12 – "Edge of the Cliff" signifies something that is impenetrable.
PAGE 13 – "The Mouths of Today's People" signifies gossiping.
PAGE 15 – "Peanuts" signifies prosperity.
PAGE 16 – "The Sickle Blade" and "Calabash Flower" signify hard work and happy family.
PAGE 19 – "My Little Secret" signifies a secret.
PAGE 20 – "Two Twisted Paths" and "Flower" signify taking different paths and harmony.
PAGE 21 – "The Talking Drum" calls warriors to battle.
PAGE 22 – "Crooked Road Walker" signifies dishonest actions.
PAGE 23 – "Belt of the Hero" signifies honor.
PAGE 25 – "Our Secret" signifies a family secret.
PAGE 26 – "Crossroads" signifies problem solving.
PAGE 29 – "Flower" signifies family harmony.

Glossary

Here are some words from the story that are in Bambara, the national language of Mali.

Dogo Zan (DOE-go ZAHN) – Brother Rabbit

Mansa Jugu (MAHN-sah JOO-goo) – greedy king (mansa means ruler; jugu means greedy)

*Ee dusu dah (ee du-SU dah) – let us bargain; calm down

*Ee ko dee (EE ko DEE) – exclamation of surprise when a person doesn't believe what they have just heard (What did you say?)

Fara (FAH-rah) – rock

*Fara-ba (FAH-rah BAH) – Mr. Rock (title of respect)

Fara doron (FAH-rah DOH-ron) – a simple rock

Moondon (MOON-don) – what is it?

Sheeyo (SHEE-yoh) – a bush with large leaves found in Mali

A toh! (ah TOH) – stop!

U-tah (OO-tah) – take it all!

*Feeyeh ku, feeyeh ku. (FEE-yeh koo) Waara sa kun tay. (WA-rah sah KOON-teh) – This is a chant of encouragement to give hope for survival in difficult times.

(Note: Bambara is a metaphorical language, so the English translation is not always literal.)

*Not a literal translation

Folkloric Cousins of *The Magic Gourd*

Stories about an object that supplies a never-ending amount of food have been popular throughout time and can be traced back to the ancient Greek mythology of the cornucopia, the horn of plenty. Two popular versions of the tale that closely resemble "The Magic Gourd" are "The Lad Who Went to the North Wind" and "The Table, the Ass, and the Stick." The strong appeal of these stories comes from the hero's acquisition of things that bring him infinite security: inexhaustible food, limitless wealth, and physical power over adversaries. There are often three objects: two that are lost or stolen and a third that recovers the first two. The hero always triumphs in the end. These satisfying tales of wish fulfillment can be found in Europe, Asia, and Africa as well as in North and South America.